Principals

by Melanie Mitchell
photographs by Stephen G. Donaldson

Lerner Publications Company • Minneapolis

Lerner Publications Company
A division of Lerner Publishing Group
241 First Avenue North
Minneapolis, MN 55401 USA

Website address: www.lernerbooks.com

Words in **bold type** are explained in a glossary on page 31.

Library of Congress Cataloging-in-Publication Data

Mitchell, Melanie (Melanie S.)
    Principals / by Melanie Mitchell.
      p.   cm. – (Pull ahead books)
    Summary: An introduction to the many jobs and responsibilities of elementary school principals.
    ISBN: 0–8225–1694–2 (lib. bdg. : alk. paper)
    1. School principals—Juvenile literature. 2. School management and organization—Juvenile literature.
[1. School principals. 2. Occupations.] I. Title. II. Series.
LB2831.9.M58 2005
371.2'012—dc22   2003023292

Manufactured in the United States of America
1 2 3 4 5 6 – JR – 10 09 08 07 06 05

"Good morning, boys and girls," says
the voice from the **loudspeaker.**
Whose voice is it?

It is the voice of the principal. The principal is the person in charge of a school.

Principals are important in the
community. Your community is made
up of people in your neighborhood,
town, or city.

Principals do many things each day.

Principals **greet** students as they get off the school bus or walk down the hallway.

Principals are in charge of everyone who works at a school.

Principals hire teachers, cooks, and **custodians.** These people help run a school.

Principals help make the rules for a school.

Sometimes principals have to talk to students about how to follow the rules.

Why is this principal reading to a group of students?

Principals help make sure students are
learning everything they need to learn
at school.

Principals also make sure students know how to stay safe while they are at school.

These students are practicing what to do in case of a **tornado.**

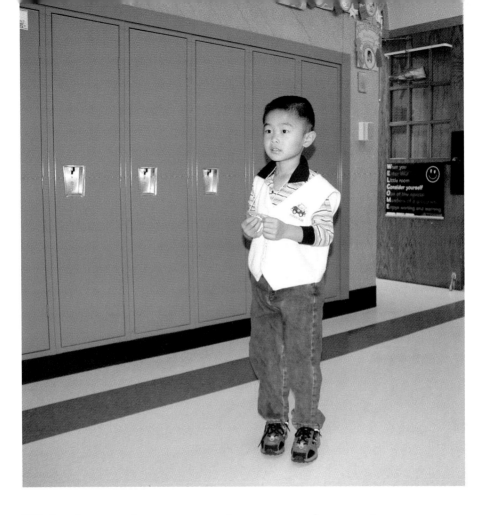

This boy does not know where to go.
Who will help him?

The principal will help. Principals are
happy to help students.

Sometimes new families move to the area. They visit the school to meet the principal.

They make sure the bills are paid to keep the school running.

Sometimes principals do fun things.
They go to school concerts and plays.

They cheer for their school's sports teams at games.

Some schools have special **goals.**
Principals help set goals.

This school
reached its
goal. This
principal is
proud of
his students.

The school day is over. The principal
says good-bye to the students.

This principal is getting ready for her next day at school!

Facts about Principals

■ People go to school to become principals. Most people study for six years or more after high school to become principals.

■ Most principals were teachers before they became principals.

■ Many principals live near the school where they work. They are important members of the community. You might have a principal living in your neighborhood.

■ A principal must be very good at working with other people. A large part of a principal's job is working with people like students, librarians, and teachers.

■ Principals at private schools are called headmasters or headmistresses.

Principals through History

■ Many years ago, schools did not have principals. The teacher did many of the jobs that principals do today. Schools are now much bigger, and principals make sure that teachers can spend all their time with their students.

■ Horace Mann is known as the father of American public schools. He made many important changes to schools more than 150 years ago. He made sure teachers were paid well and that they had good rooms to teach students in. Mann also wanted teachers to learn how to best teach students. Principals began working at schools to make sure teachers were doing the best job they could.

■ The oldest wooden school building in the United States is in St. Augustine, Florida. It was built over 200 years ago! There was no principal at this school. The teacher was in charge of the school.

More about Principals

Check out these books and websites to find out more about principals. Or stop by your school's office and talk to the principal!

Books

Doudna, Kelly. *School around the World.* Edina, MN: SandCastle, 2004.

Nelson, Robin. *Being a Leader.* Minneapolis: Lerner Publications Company, 2003.

Nelson, Robin. *School Then and Now.* Minneapolis: Lerner Publications Company, 2003.

Weber, Valerie, and Gloria Jenkins. *School in Grandma's Day.* Minneapolis: Carolrhoda Books, Inc., 1999.

Websites

National Association of Elementary School Principals
http://www.naesp.org/

Only a Teacher
http://www.pbs.org/onlyateacher/

Remembering the Little Red Schoolhouse
http://www.americaslibrary.gov/cgi-bin/page.cgi/es/mn/schlhse_1

Glossary

community: a group of people who live in the same city, town, or neighborhood. Communities share the same fire departments, schools, libraries, and other helpful places.

custodians: people who take care of buildings

goals: things wanted or worked for

greet: to welcome someone

loudspeaker: a machine that makes sound louder

tornado: a storm with very fast, spinning wind

Index

Photo Acknowledgments

Additional photographs appear courtesy of: © Todd Strand/Independent Picture Service, front cover, pp. 4, 8, 21, 27; © Beth Johnson/Independent Picture Service, pp. 5, 6, 12, 20; PhotoDisc Royalty Free by Getty Images, p. 23; © Erin Liddell/Independent Picture Service, p. 24; The Denver Public Library, p. 29.